All the World

written by liz garton scanlon

and

illustrated by marla frazee

Beach Lane Books

New York   London   Toronto   Sydney

For Kirk—L.G.S.

For Reed—M.F.

BEACH LANE BOOKS

An imprint of Simon & Schuster Children's Publishing Division

1230 Avenue of the Americas, New York, New York 10020

Text copyright © 2009 by Elizabeth Garton Scanlon

Illustrations copyright © 2009 by Marla Frazee

All rights reserved, including the right of reproduction in whole or in part in any form.

BEACH LANE BOOKS is a trademark of Simon & Schuster, Inc.

Book design by Marla Frazee

The text for this book is hand-lettered by Marla Frazee.

The illustrations for this book are rendered in black Prismacolor pencil

and watercolors on Strathmore 2-ply hotpress paper.

Manufactured in the United States of America

15

Library of Congress Cataloging-in-Publication Data

Scanlon, Elizabeth Garton.

All the world / Liz Garton Scanlon ; illustrated by Marla Frazee.—1st ed.

p. cm.

ISBN: 978-1-4169-8580-8 (hardcover : alk. paper)

1. Children's poetry, American. I. Frazee, Marla, ill. II. Title.

PS3619.C265A79 2009

811'.6—dc22

2008051057

0316 PCH

Rock,
stone,
pebble,
sand

Body, shoulder, arm, hand

A moat to dig,

a shell
to keep

All the world is wide and deep

Hive, bee, wings, hum

Husk, cob, corn,

yum!

Tomato blossom,
         fruit so red

All the world's a garden bed

Tree, trunk,
branch,
crown

Climbing up and sitting down

Morning sun becomes noon-blue

All the world
is old and new

Road, street, track, path

Ship, boat, wooden raft

Nest, bird, feather, fly

All the world has
got its sky

Slip, trip, stumble, fall
Tip the bucket, spill it all

Better luck
another
day

All the world

goes round this way

Table, bowl,
cup, spoon

Hungry tummy,
supper's soon

Butter, flour, big black pot

All the world
is cold and hot

Spreading
shadows,
setting sun

Crickets, curtains, day is done

A fire
takes
away the
chill

Nanas,
papas,
cousins, kin   Piano, harp,

and violin   Babies passed from neck to knee

Everything you hear, smell, see

All the world is everything

Everything is you and me

and love and trust

All the
world

is
all of
us